PRAISE FOR
A SEARCH FOR SAFE PASSAGE

Why did the bear cross the road? Author Frances Figart answers this question for young readers in this story of companionship and adventure. Through the journey of a variety of likeable forest animals, concepts of road ecology and the effect of highways on wildlife movement are introduced in a simple, understandable manner. This book gives young influencers the tools to impact how we as a society address highway wildlife mortality in the future.

~Terry McGuire, retired highway engineer,
Parks Canada

A Search for Safe Passage *is a very accessible introduction to the problems and solutions associated with highways, traffic, and wildlife. Through easily understandable stories of the animal characters, we learn that cars can kill animals, and that a busy highway can also be a barrier to the search for food, water, mates, and new areas to live. The stories of the animals in this book also show that different species have different requirements for safe crossing opportunities. Kids quickly understand the principles... they get it!... and so can adults!*

~Marcel Huijser, PhD, road ecologist,
wildlife biologist

In this imaginative and beautifully illustrated book, Frances Figart offers a delightful cast of wild characters—and allows us to see our world through an animal's eyes. Her story of their journey to find a safe passage over a dangerous highway helps us understand the perilous and often deadly threats our roads pose to animals everywhere, and provides insight into the ways we as humans can solve this problem by building wildlife crossings.

~Beth Pratt, author of *When Mountain Lions Are Neighbors* and leader of the National Wildlife Federation's #SaveLACougars campaign

Frances pulls back the underbrush and provides a glimpse into the secretive world of wildlife that inhabit the forests near Interstate 40, just outside the boundary of Great Smoky Mountains National Park. She brings to light a real-world problem—and potential solutions—from the perspective of the critters. This is a great book whose time has come!

~Jeff Hunter, Senior Program Manager, National Parks Conservation Association

A SEARCH FOR SAFE PASSAGE

A SEARCH FOR SAFE PASSAGE

by Frances Figart

illustrations by Emma DuFort

1 2 3 4 5 6 7 8 9 10

Published by Great Smoky Mountains Association
ISBN 978-0-937207-01-7
Printed in the USA

All purchases benefit Great Smoky Mountains Association, a private,
nonprofit organization that supports the educational, scientific, and
historical programs of Great Smoky Mountains National Park.

for Taylor Barnhill
who provoked me to write this book

John Beaudet
through whom the love and support
of my parents lives on

and to all the human beings
working across the globe to help animals
find safer ways to cross our roads

TABLE OF CONTENTS

CHAPTER 1 Danger on the Human Highway   1

CHAPTER 2 Discovering the Black Hole   9

CHAPTER 3 Meeting of the Forest Council   16

CHAPTER 4 Strangers Extend an Invitation   22

CHAPTER 5 Journey to a Secret Passage   30

CHAPTER 6 A Traveler Tells of a Landbridge   38

CHAPTER 7 New Friends Along the Way   48

CHAPTER 8 Reunion on the Landbridge   57

MEET THE REAL ANIMALS   70

HOW TO HELP THEM CROSS   92

INFLUENCES, ALLUSIONS, AND THANKS   102

SAFE PASSAGE: ANIMALS NEED A HAND (SONG)   106

ABOUT THE AUTHOR AND ILLUSTRATOR   110

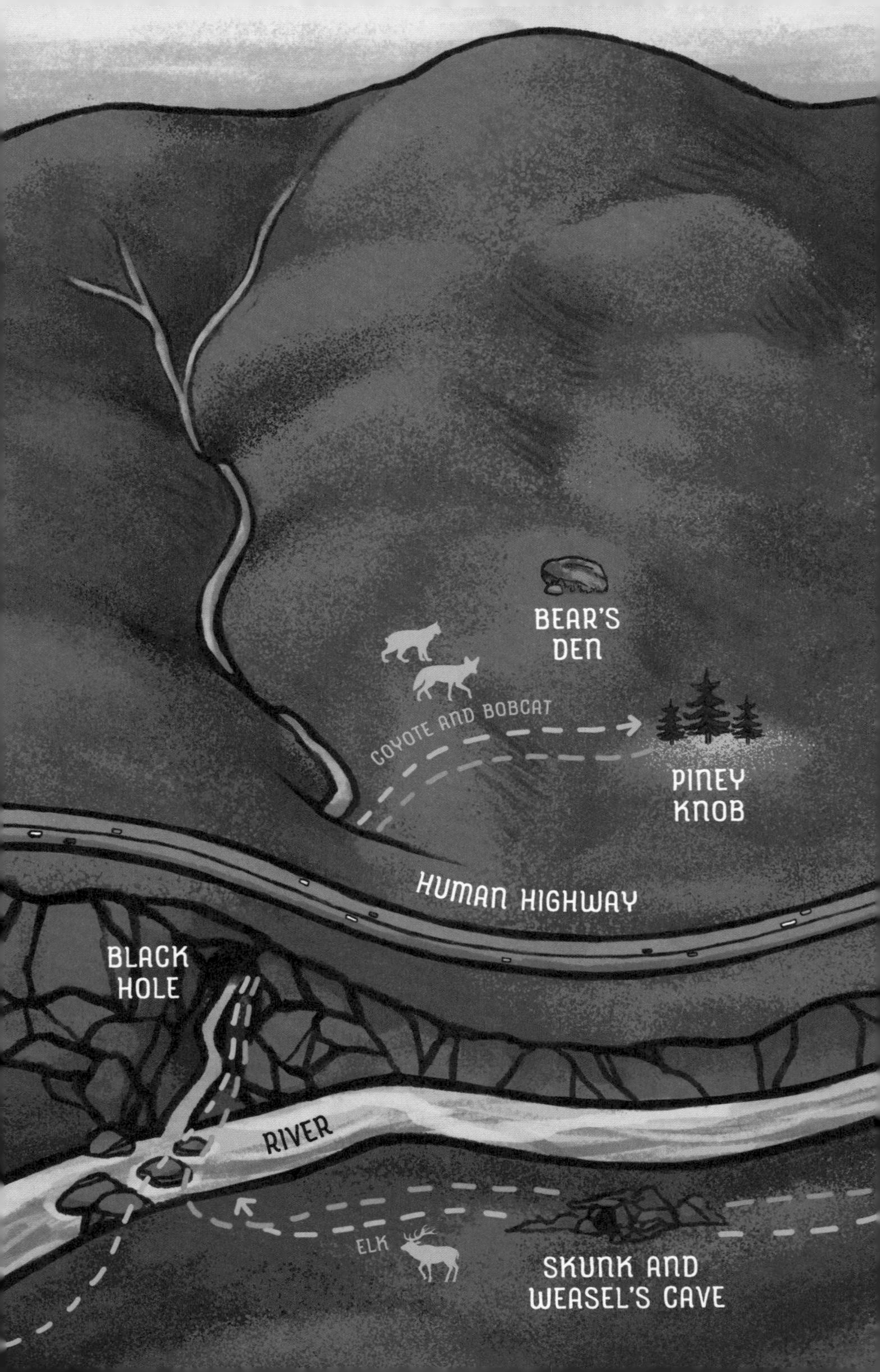
BEAR'S DEN
COYOTE AND BOBCAT
PINEY KNOB
HUMAN HIGHWAY
BLACK HOLE
RIVER
ELK
SKUNK AND WEASEL'S CAVE

N

W E

S

THE GORGE

LANDBRIDGE

GROUP FROM NORTH

CHAPTER 1
Danger on the Human Highway

Bear awoke in late afternoon. His nose was always the first part of him to wake up, while the rest of him remained quite drowsy.

First, he could smell the earthen scent of the warm, moist leaves and dark soil of his little den—a slightly sunken spot behind a big moss-covered grey rock just below the ridgetop of a steep mountain. Then he could smell the fragrance of all kinds of blossoms blooming near his home— white, pink, purple and yellow ones. Next he could smell sweet, juicy insect larvae in the rotting logs around his den, the musky aroma of mushrooms ripening, and his favorite snacks: white oak acorns and bear corn. And today, there was a different scent, something he didn't quite recognize, but he knew it gave him a new kind of springy energy.

He opened his eyes and saw the sun was getting low in the sky. His best friend Deer would most likely already be on the Piney Knob just over on the other side of the ridge to get the news report from Hawk. Tonight was a big night. The moon would be full, and the Forest Council would be meeting. So, he lumbered up, yawned, stretched his body out long, shook out his coat from head to toe, scratched his back by moving up and down on his very own scratch tree, snuffled up some acorns and set off to climb the ridge to the very tip top.

Thrushes were singing their flute-like songs on the tip top of the ridge, where Bear could look down into the whole wide valley below. Way down at the very bottom, he could just barely make out the river gleaming in the last of the sun's light. Beside it, though he couldn't really see it well, he could hear and smell the thing that terrified him more than anything ever had terrified him in his life.

Bear's home was a beautiful gorge formed long ago and ringed by tall mountains with ridges, rocks, streams, trees of all kinds, and lots of animals on either side—and with a swift, rocky river constantly rushing far below. Bear's ancestors had roamed freely from one side of the gorge to the other, getting anything and everything they wanted to eat and finding the best mates to keep them company.

Back in the time of Bear's grandparents, Humans had built the Human Highway that now divided the gorge into the North and the South. Bear lived in the North. He had always wanted to go to the South, but there were many reasons why he had decided he would never even try to cross over.

He could see the Piney Knob a little ways farther down the mountain slope and make out the shape of Deer and some other smaller animals with her. It looked like Woodchuck, who was usually there this time of day, and his latest fan, the young Squirrel. Bear bounded down the mountainside to join them.

"Hey, Beast!" Bear said cheerfully as he tumbled onto the Piney Knob. "Hey Beast!" Deer answered him back with a sweet smile.

Since they were little, the two friends had greeted each other this way. Bear and Deer had been born around the same time, two years ago. Once, when they were playing too close to Skunk's place, Bear's mom had scolded them and said they should "stay away from that filthy beast." Bear, at that time just a baby, had asked, "Why do you call him that? Is a beast something bad?" Mother Bear had said, "No, it's good to be a beast; I just don't want you two to upset that striped Skunk, or he'll stink up the whole hillside." Baby Bear and Deer had found this so funny that they just kept using the name Beast as their secret joke.

Here on the Piney Knob, Deer was browsing on blueberries and huckleberries. Woodchuck was grazing, and Squirrel was foraging. Bear tried to forage as well, but his heart just wasn't in it. Although Deer really liked munching here, Bear always felt very nervous on this spot.

From here, he could more clearly see, hear, and, worst of all, *smell* the Human Highway. It was full of huge, racing, noisy, metal boxes with wheels that steamed and groaned and honked and moaned and sent forth all sorts of foul-smelling gasses. Plus, the Humans dropped all kinds of tempting food along the side of the road—food that had attracted Bear's mother. The awful noise and horrible smell made his heart beat faster, his stomach go all queasy, and his head spin so much that he felt he would surely pass out. He opened his mouth and huffed.

In spite of feeling sick, Bear couldn't shake the really strong feeling that he needed to cross to the South. He felt so afraid of the Human Highway, yet he felt it was so important that he go to the other side. Bear and the other animals on the North side believed that the ones in the South had more plentiful food and water than they did. The river was on the South side, so the animals over there seemed stronger and healthier and had shinier coats. Bear felt like some ancient memory or secret code was pushing him to go over. And there only seemed to be the one way—to cross where his parents had crossed before him, and where their parents had crossed before them, and . . .

"Make way," a voice shrieked from above them—and suddenly there was a tremendous rush of air and a grand fluttering of wings. It was Hawk, who had just flown over the Human Highway from the South and now came in

for an impressive, if somewhat intrusive, landing on the Piney Knob. Bear, Deer, Woodchuck, and Squirrel all jumped back to the edge of the knob to make room for Hawk's huge wings, shoots and berries and other nibblings dropping from their gaping mouths.

"Traffic and weather report," cried Hawk in his squawky voice that always seemed to Bear to be more piercing than necessary. "Worst of the rush hour has passed. Storm brewing way out to the Southeast. Should get here before sunrise if it stays on course."

"Why thank you, Hawk," said Woodchuck, standing up to get a better view of the goings-on below. "If the traffic is getting lighter, and that does appear to be true, then I'm going to go on down where the grass is greener. Everyone knows the grazing is best right beside the Human Highway. Anyone care to join me?"

Woodchuck was known to be something of a ham, which was probably why some called him Groundhog. He was old enough to know better, but he liked to play daredevil by nibbling as close as possible to the Human Highway while the huge metal boxes with wheels raced by just inches from his show-off nose. And if he could have an audience, all the better, as Woodchuck was never one to be alone for very long.

"You know our stance," said Bear, moving closer to Deer. "We've vowed not to even go near the Human Highway anymore, much less try to cross, and we don't feel that you should take any chances either."

"Yes," agreed Deer, "and, in fact, I beg you not to go down there because I've had the odd feeling all day that something bad is about to happen."

"Simple matter of policy," Hawk squawked. "Mustn't go because of the danger. All have agreed to Turtle's Law in the Forest Council: it's for our own welfare to stay away!"

"I'll go with you, Woodchuck," said Squirrel a bit nervously, ignoring everyone's advice. "The traffic does seem to be thinning out and slowing down a bit, and there are really good things for us to eat right beside the Human Highway."

6

"Aw, c'mon guys, don't be a buzz kill," Woodchuck said, throwing his head back and rolling his eyes toward the sky, showing his prominent front teeth. "I'm just staying on the shoulder, as usual. Come on if you're coming, Squirrel."

Squirrel looked up at the others for a moment and then back at Woodchuck. Her conflict was obvious. "I'd like to go, but maybe I really shouldn't. But then again, at the same time, I love an adventure, and I don't want you to go alone, Woodchuck."

Then without more ado, the two smaller animals bounded rapidly down the mountain while Bear, Deer, and Hawk looked on disapprovingly.

"Don't forget: Forest Council meeting right here when the moon is high!" cried Hawk after them. But they were already long gone.

"I'm not too worried about Woodchuck," said Bear. "He's actually pretty careful and knows what he's doing. But that Squirrel is young and inexperienced, and she can be . . . well, kind of squirrely."

They were silent for a while, tasting the juicy berries, feeling the wind on their faces, listening to the Thrushes, and basking in the last glow of sunlight.

"Wind's picking up," Hawk observed.

"Will you be presiding tonight, Hawk?" asked Deer, respectfully.

"Owl will lead," he replied. "Night's more her time."

"Have the two of you found any new—?" Bear's question

trailed off as they all heard a sharp whistle and a squeaking, squealing noise from down on the Human Highway.

Hawk immediately raised his wings and took off in the direction of the sounds. Looking down, Bear and Deer could make out the figure of Groundhog standing up and peering out into the traffic. But where was young Squirrel?

Bear and Deer watched as Hawk circled the West-bound lane of metal boxes with wheels, still speeding along.

"What can we do about the Human Highway?" asked Deer. "First it took your mom, then mine!"

"I know," said Bear. "We would still be with our moms if only . . . Well, at least we have each other. But you know, what's really weird is, I am convinced that my soul mate is over there on the other side, and I'll never reach her, I'll never find her. I may never find someone to share my scratch tree with."

Hawk was now flying back toward them, sailing on the strong winds that come before a storm. They anxiously waited for his report. But as he glided over the Piney Knob, Hawk didn't cry out as usual. He only angled his left wing slightly downward from his body, signaling bad news.

CHAPTER 2
Discovering the Black Hole

"I've searched my assigned territory thoroughly," Coyote was saying in the most confident reporting voice he could muster. "I've traveled over five square miles, crossed 13 creeks and branches and even the river a few times, scouted four black holes (two round and two square)—but, alas, they were either too small to enter or did not lead to the other side. I've basically got nothing positive to report in the way of a passage."

On the South side, Coyote and his friend Bobcat were on a mission. Both of them were really tired and frustrated. They had been traveling for weeks now, searching tirelessly and unwilling to give up. They were looking for a way to get from the South to the North without crossing the Human Highway.

And this was very odd because they were the experts at crossing it. For several years, they had crossed together many nights with their red-haired buddy and guide, Fox, who taught them all his tricks when they hung out with him on their rocky outcrop above the Human Highway. Fox was a little older than they were, super smart, funny, and adored by them both. The three of them had the best of times together in those days. They got to eat everything they wanted, and they all had lots of luck with dating.

But a couple of months ago, during an unexpectedly foggy crossing, Fox—the one who knew the most and taught them everything about being safe—had suddenly been killed by a speeding metal box with wheels. And, just like that, all their good times were over.

Losing their charming, intelligent mentor had made Bobcat and Coyote very sad. For weeks they didn't see one another, both slept too much, and neither ate well. But after this period of grieving, they met up one night and realized their shared loss had made the bond between them stronger. Up on the rocky outcrop where they had all hung out so many times, the two held a secret ceremony for Fox and made a pact in his name never to cross the Human Highway again until they had tried everything in their power to find another, safer way to get to the other side.

Unlikely friends, a cat and a dog, Bobcat and Coyote were different in some ways, but actually they were a lot alike. Coyote liked being in charge, determining their plan, setting their daily goals, and leading the way. Though quieter and more independent, Bobcat was just as obsessed with their mission and determined to uphold their vow. They were both logical, mature, and confident—not unlike their memory of Fox, which constantly inspired them. All the skills they had learned and practiced in crossing the Human Highway were now being used in their quest to find a safe alternative.

Staying on the South side, they were slowly moving their way East, following the river's path, making a new camp every couple of days, resting a while when the sun was high, then splitting up in the afternoon to scout the area for possible passages, often searching throughout the night. Each morning, a little before sunrise, just as the last of the Whippoorwills called, they returned to camp to report on their findings—or lack thereof.

"I think I may have found something," Bobcat was now saying in her quietest, silky-soft low voice.

"Oh," said Coyote, surprised and excited. "Cool!"

"C'mon," she said. "I'll show you. It's a black hole about a mile from here, and it's larger than the usual ones."

It's pretty high up, and I'm not sure we can reach it, she thought, but didn't say that part out loud.

After bounding across a boulder-strewn section of the river, Bobcat led Coyote through a deep gulch in the mountainside and then up, up, up through a rhododendron thicket to a faint trail beside a tiny creek. Coyote watched Bobcat's cute tail bobbing in front of his nose and felt tired and grumpy. He didn't like following; he liked to be in the lead. Bobcat felt nervous because she knew the opening of the hole was high off the ground and it had water flowing right out of it! Bobcat didn't like getting her paws wet. Plus, she wasn't sure she could even reach the opening.

Whippoorwills sang in the trees above them as they followed the faint trail along the tiny creek for a long time. Finally, the creek made a big turn and got narrower, and the bank got steeper. And there, emptying a trickle of water into the creek, was a large black hole—a round tunnel-like structure marked with a circular pattern of ridges that was framed by the same hard grey stone-like stuff that made up the Human Highway.

Bobcat and Coyote looked at each other, their eyes wide.

"Could it be a passage to the other side?" she asked him.

"Did you not test it already?" Coyote inquired.

Bobcat looked down. "I couldn't actually make it up into the opening without getting . . . well, you know, wet."

"Ah, Bobbie!" Coyote flashed her a toothy grin. "C'mon. I'll help you."

And with that he leapt up onto the round structure with a single, graceful movement, creating a splash that echoed for what sounded like a long way. That intrigued them both.

"Now, just come over here to my left and jump up,"

Coyote said, "and I'll keep you from landing in the water."

Bobcat edged over close to the hole. Standing up, she used her left paw to grab hold of the bottom of the hole where it sloped up, and she placed her right paw inside the hole where Coyote stood and helped to stabilize it. From there she tried to hoist herself up, but the opening seemed too high.

"I'm too low. I'm not tall enough," Bobcat growled.

"No, you're fine," Coyote insisted. "Now you've just got to take those fluffy back feet of yours off the ground."

But this was too scary. Bobcat hissed in disgust.

"Do it, Bobbie!" Coyote commanded now. "Or I'm going on in without you."

Coyote stepped farther into the opening, but Bobcat could still see his eyes shining in the half-darkness. She felt exhausted and irritable. Why was he calling her Bobbie? The only one who had ever called her that was . . .

Fox! Bobcat's memory flashed on an image of their old ginger-haired friend, lying lifeless on the cold, grey Human Highway. Suddenly every hair on her body stood on end—and she knew what she had to do.

Bobcat let her back feet come off the ground and lifted them up to the underneath of the black hole. At the same time, she moved her left paw from outside to inside the hole. With all four paws in place, but just barely, she held onto the slippery surface as if her life depended on it. Then she lifted her body with her strong forelegs and

scratched off with her back feet against the ridges on the outside of the hole. On the first desperate attempt, she almost slipped back out of the opening. But then, with her back feet dug in, she pushed even harder and kicked off with all her might. She was in!

"Listen!" Coyote whispered. "Can you hear it?"

Not only could she hear it, Bobcat could feel it—the muted rumbling of hundreds of huge, terrible somethings passing over what now appeared most certainly to be a long tunnel. They must be under the Human Highway!

CHAPTER 3
Meeting of the Forest Council

Bear was dreaming of ants. There was a rotting log full of them, and he was digging them out with his sharp claws and scooping them into his mouth. He wanted to keep eating them in his dream, but something was making him wake up. A light was shining in his eyes.

The moon! Bear sat straight up. The full moon was high in the sky and shining into his den—the Forest Council meeting would be starting soon. "Late again," he huffed, and he lumbered up, fluffed up his coat with a total body shake, and scratched his back twice on his scratch tree for good measure. He snuffled up a handful of real ants from the rotting log nearby and headed up the slope toward the ridgetop.

As he scaled the ridge and then sauntered down toward the Piney Knob, Bear was relieved to hear and smell that now there was much less traffic down on the Human Highway.

16

His friends were standing, sitting, or lying around in a circle, and Owl was already calling the roll. Bear slipped into the circle between Deer and Snake. Bear liked Snake a lot, even though he was very old, slithered and writhed around, and always smelled like cucumber, so no one else was sitting right next to him. "Beast!" Bear whispered to Deer. She gave him a look that said: *You're late, but I'm happy to see you.* "Beast," she said in a hushed tone.

"Deer?" Owl called. "Here," said Deer.

"Firefly?" "Nearby."

"Frog?" "Present and accounted for."

"Hawk?" "Standing by."

"Possum?" "Present. And, um, it's Opossum."

"Raccoon?" "Here."

"Salamander?" "*Pseudotriton ruber*, at your service," said Salamander, who liked to use her scientific name at meetings.

"Snake?" "Yesssssss . . . ?" asked Snake, as if he had forgotten something. "Oh, yessss of coursssssse, I'm here."

"Squirrel?"

There was an awkward silence, and the full moon was beginning to make its slow descent toward the top of the ridge.

"Won't be coming," said Hawk in a somewhat judgmental squawk.

"And it's all my fault," muttered Woodchuck, who had just arrived and looked rather downtrodden and terribly guilty. Bear and Deer exchanged a knowing glance.

"Alright," said Owl, "let me finish calling the roll, and then we will talk about what has occurred. Bear, I have already called your name, and I see by the light of this beautiful full moon that you are now here. Turtle?"

"Yes... I'm... um... just... barely... here," said Turtle in a weak, gurgley voice. Like Snake, she was also very old and, apparently, out of breath from traveling uphill to the meeting.

"Now, Woodchuck," said Owl, "you may proceed with your account of this afternoon's incident."

"Wait!" said Opossum confidently, then added more shyly: "Shouldn't you call his name so he can say that he is here first?"

"Oh, yes, okay, alright," Owl said, slightly flustered. "Woodchuck?"

"I'm here," said Woodchuck gloomily.

"Please tell us what happened," Deer said sympathetically.

"We were just munching and nibbling," Woodchuck began. "I wasn't paying attention really, and all of a sudden Squirrel darted out into the Human Highway. I think she saw some of those golden, salty sticks the Humans drop. I leaned toward the traffic and whistled really loud like this: *Wheet!* Too late, she realized her mistake and panicked. I heard some squeaking and squealing, and then Squirrel was tumbling, twisting, turning—and then I just don't know what all happened. I closed my eyes until it was over."

Woodchuck was now sobbing. Owl put a large wing around him.

"There, there, Woodchuck," Owl said soothingly. "We've all seen this happen, and it's never easy. That's why Hawk and I have been doing our scouting missions. Even though *we* can *fly*, the Human Highway has taken some of *our* ancestors too. So, we want to help all of you who are on foot to find a safe passage."

"Ahem," Snake murmured.

"Ah, yes," said Owl, "and we want to help those of you who are not on foot, as well."

"Normally many of us would naturally be at odds with one another," said Frog, "but we're all working together as a team to find a solution for everyone."

Owl nodded. "It's been almost a year since we passed Turtle's Law, in effect making it the policy of the Forest Council *not* to cross the Human Highway."

Turtle chimed in, pleased she'd been mentioned. "As a result of that law (*my* law), um, we have basically given up the part of our territory that is now in the South, which has left us, um, with fewer food and water options."

"Yet some," Owl continued, "have violated the law, and we have seen the sad consequences even here tonight."

Listening to this discussion, Bear began to feel restless. He realized he was pacing, his mind racing, because he was beginning to feel a desperate sense of dread. It was as if his life's purpose was never going to be fulfilled.

"But we can't give up yet," he said, in a huffing voice. "There must be some way to get back and forth between the North and the South without having to cross the Human Highway."

"There is!" said a strange voice from the ridgetop. Everyone looked up in that direction. There, illumnated by the descending full moon, were two huge, strange, lean, mean silhouettes.

CHAPTER 4
Strangers Extend an Invitation

There was a muffled commotion on the Piney Knob while the smaller animals in the Forest Council instinctively moved behind the larger ones.

Bear whispered to Deer: "I don't like the look of these suspicious characters. Let's assume the position."

"Okay," said Deer, "but for some reason I think they may surprise us in a good way."

Bear and Deer took three steps toward the strangers. At the same instant, Hawk settled on Bear's shoulders, and Owl flew up to perch on Deer's back. Both birds raised their wings, puffed up their bodies, and fluffed out their feathers, trying to appear as large and scary as possible. Everyone else stayed behind this defense formation, which the animals had practiced many times.

"Whooooooo are you?" asked Owl in her most authoritative tone.

"State your business here," Hawk cried out, his shriek piercing the air.

The two newcomers stepped forward a bit, and, amid some murmuring, the smaller animals in the Forest Council nestled in closer behind their leaders.

"I am Coyote," said the thinner one, sounding a bit put off by the group's suspicions.

"And I am Bobcat," said the fluffier one in a silky, low voice. "We are here in friendship. We come from the South."

"Yes, I can see by your coat, my friend, you're from the other side," said Deer politely, hoping to bring harmony with a compliment.

"We couldn't help but overhear your discussion of seeking safe passage," said Bobcat.

"We have no intention to harm you," Coyote said reassuringly. "We lost a good friend on the Human Highway West of here, and we have been traveling for weeks in search of a better way to cross."

Owl and Hawk swiveled their heads to look at one another. Bear raised his nose to sniff the wind as if questioning the strangers' intentions, but Deer nodded her approval. All four of them looked back toward the visitors.

"Come and join us," said Owl, as she and Hawk glided down to the ground and used their outspread wings to direct the group to make a circle once again—only this time wide enough for everyone to sit with plenty of physical distance in between each other.

Bobcat and Coyote advanced. They didn't look nearly so large when they had stepped out of the moon's light. To seem less threatening, they politely parted, choosing seats on opposite sides of the circle. In hopes of helping the other animals feel protected, Bear and Owl sat on either side of Coyote, while Hawk and Deer flanked Bobcat.

"Because we don't all know each other well," began Owl, "let's go around the circle and introduce ourselves. I will start. I am Owl, and I take on the role of teacher. I'm passionate about creating positive change and helping everyone reach their potential."

Owl then swiveled her head to the right to prompt the next speaker, Frog, who then suddenly jumped up in the air and seemed to fly over the heads of Salamander and Turtle, landing up high on a group of nearby rocks.

"I'm just Frog, and I help out Owl and everyone on the team with whatever they need," he croaked, hopping to the next rock. "I like to be active," he continued, hopping to another rock, "and I turn work into play." He concluded with another flying leap back over Turtle and Salamander and down to his spot on the Piney Knob.

"I'm Salamander, *Pseudotriton ruber*, the Red Salamander to be specific (ruber means red)," said Salamander excitedly, "and I like to explain things, and I can be in water for a long time because I can breathe through my skin, and, and, and I can even regenerate parts of my body if something happens to them."

"I am Turtle," said the group's oldest member. "I was born in this gorge in the time before the Human Highway, and with my parents I traveled the ancient trail that it disturbed. Our territory used to extend over to the South, but, um, now we have become restricted to the North side only. I've seen so many of my kin killed on that death trap that I never go there anymore, and I helped to institute a law that this council all consider the Human Highway off limits."

"I'm Sssssnake, and I'm almosssst as old as Turtle," Snake said, writhing and slithering around as he spoke. "My parentsss were here when the Human Highway was built. I am the healer, the keeper of Nature'ssssss medisssssss-cine. Once, we freely roamed this land, but now we are nearly rubbed out. Eat what you have clossssse by, I ssssssay. Find matesssss here in the North. Traveling will sssssurely bring our downfall." He ended his speech with a loud, dry rattle, a sound he made only when he was frightened or very passionate about something.

Next, a tiny, squeaky poem came out of the darkness, and a lantern came on just as the little character uttered the last word of each of his lines:

"Firefly is my *name*,
and light is my *game*.
I do not speak most of the *time*,
but when I do, I make a *rhyme*."

"I am Deer, and I'm pretty quiet too," said Deer, in a voice that sounded like a smile. "I want peace, harmony, and to help everyone find safe passage. I believe it exists."

Next in the circle was one of the strangers: "I'm Bobcat, and I'm happy to know all of you. I like to use my strategic thinking for good outcomes."

"Hawk here," the next council member squawked. "With my ability to fly, I used to try to guide others across the Human Highway. But I have learned the hard way that it's not safe for anyone to cross anymore, and so I'm hopeful we can find safe passage."

"I am Raccoon, and like Deer, I want harmony between all animals—and even with the Human Beings. I believe that if they really knew us, they would never build something like the Human Highway. I also brought us all some mushrooms, blueberries, and huckleberries." And with that she proceeded to go around the circle, carrying her offerings in her little hands, and placing some food in front of each member of the Forest Council, giving extra to their guests. "These have all been washed," she concluded.

"I'm Woodchuck and I, I, I think my nose is bleeding," said Woodchuck and fell over backwards dramatically. "It

got scraped on the Human Highway when I was whistling for Squirrel." They could no longer see him, but his voice kept on talking. "I may need some something medicinally speaking, Snake!"

"Let me ssssssssssssseeeee," hissed Snake. He slithered across the Piney Knob to Woodchuck, inspected his nose, then writhed around in the vegetation nearby collecting medicinal herbs. As the others munched on Raccoon's snacks, Snake prepared and administered the herbs to the wounded Woodchuck. Opossum was watching the entire process when she realized it was time for her introduction.

27

"I am Opossum. I love history, and I do not really do well with change. I tend to just freeze and pretend to be dead rather than face my fear. I can't go to the Human Highway anymore because I've seen my parents, my sister and my brothers all killed there. It's traumatic. So, I realize we do need to find an alternative."

Bear took a deep breath. He was still feeling suspicious but wanted to trust the newcomers as Deer seemed to do. "I'm Bear, and I'm beginning to feel that today is one of great significance," he said. "If these strangers have some information that will help us, I believe we should let them tell us about it."

"I'm Coyote and we can do you one better than that," said Coyote. "Now that we all know each other better, would you like us to lead you to the black hole by which we traveled here from the South? We'll not only show it to you, but Bobcat and I can be your tour guides on the other side. Our goal is to train every species to use this tunnel passage and to be able to share it with others."

"How far away is it?" asked Salamander.

"How big is it?" asked Bear.

"It's only a couple of hours away," answered Bobcat. "And it may be big enough for even you, Bear. It's the biggest one we've found."

"Then why haven't we seen it before?" asked Bear under his breath, still somewhat skeptical.

"It's well hidden in a rhododendron thicket," said

Coyote, who had good hearing, "so it would have easily escaped your notice."

"I think we should at least all go and see it," said Deer, encouraging Bear to think positively. "The trip itself will be fun."

"Agreed," cried Hawk.

"Yes," said Owl, "we should." She looked at Frog, who was already hopping up and down at the prospect of an adventure.

"Um, some of us move slowly and have to take our time over long distances," said Turtle.

"Indeed," said Snake.

"I can carry you, Turtle," said Raccoon, holding out her little hands, palms upturned.

"And I can carry you, Snake, and you as well, Salamander," said Opossum, patting the small pouch in her belly and waving her eerie tail, which actually could hold onto things.

"Thanks, Possum," said Salamander.

"You are welcome, and it's Opossum," she corrected.

"Then follow me, but first gather up what food you can," said Coyote. "You're going to need your strength."

With the full moon still high enough to shine some light on their path, the group set out with Coyote leading and Bobcat bringing up the rear.

CHAPTER 5
Journey to a Secret Passage

Coyote led the group up, up, up to a high ridgetop. They had always seen this ridge and considered it the western border of their territory, but other than Bear and Deer—who had sneaked off to play up here when very young—no one in their group had ever explored it before. The higher they got, the more moonlight they had to light their way.

Bear and Deer were like kids again, enjoying this unexpected trek in the middle of the night. Hawk and Owl flew some and walked some with the group. Owl was in her element, but Hawk—who normally slept at night and forced himself to get up early for these important Forest Council meetings—found his feathers a bit ruffled.

Frog hopped in and out of the lineup, encouraging everyone to keep their spirits up, especially Woodchuck, who was by now in a rather foul mood, his nose greasy with Snake's stinky medicines. Turtle put herself in high gear to keep up, and Raccoon carried her for a while when she got tired. Opossum carried Snake and Salamander—along with quite a few blueberries and huckleberries squeezed in between them—in her pouch. Bobcat and Firefly brought up the rear.

Within an hour's time, they had traveled down the other side of the western ridge and found themselves in completely new territory—on a rough trail beside a little creek that wound its way down through a rhododendron thicket, just as Coyote had described. Bobcat had explained (to those who could hear her soft, silky voice in the rear of the line) that, from this northern end, the black hole would be down low, close to the ground, and easy to get into. But on the South side, where they had come from, there was a steep drop off.

Bear and Deer followed Coyote around a bend in the trail and emerged into a small clearing edged with large boulders, and right in front of them was the black hole! Bear suddenly felt disoriented. The moon had gone down, and though the faint glow of predawn was starting to show, it was quite dark down here under all this brush. The boulders looked like great big scary creatures. He could hear or feel a rumbling too, and it made him dizzy.

"Give me some air," said Bear breathlessly.

Deer peered into the blackness of the hole. "So . . . this is actually a tunnel that leads to the South?" she asked Coyote.

"Yes," he said, "and Bobbie, uh, Bobcat discovered it."

All the animals came into the little clearing to see the black hole for the first time. Snake and Salamander were anxious to get out of Opossum's pouch for a while. Raccoon handed out berries, and there was much chatter all around.

Bear had never felt so conflicted in his entire life. Finally, here was his chance to go across safely to the other side—to the South! But he couldn't see his paw in front of his face, and it was going to be a very tight fit. He felt afraid.

He could only remember one other time he had been so scared. That was when his mother had led him out onto the Human Highway when he was only a year old. He had wanted to follow her, but he was terrified. And then, his whole life changed in an instant. Mother Bear got hit by a metal box with wheels. Though badly hurt, she was able to drag herself into the forest on the North side, where he stayed with her until she died. That was when he went to live with Deer and her mother.

Now the rumbling seemed to come from all around him, and Bear wanted to run. He looked at Deer for reassurance. Her eyes looked sad.

Finally, Owl hooted for everyone to settle down. They all gazed up at Bear and noticed he was huffing and shaking.

"I'm afraid. I can't see well enough," he said. "I don't think I can go through such a small and black, black hole."

A hush fell over the group of friends. It was as if everyone shared his fear.

"Silly Bear, be not aff*right*.
I will guide you with my *light*."

A tiny voice came out of the darkness, with a bright flash at the end of each line of poetry.

It was Firefly, of course, zooming up to light on Bear's head. And as this tiny, friendly creature landed upon him, Bear realized that the rumbling he had heard was only thunder. Suddenly lightning flashed all around them. These things were reassuring to Bear—he had always loved storms.

Now he knew that everything was right with the world. This was his destiny. He would go. He would cross over to the South and find his soul mate at last. And although he might never again return to his little den below the ridgetop with his very own scratch tree and his white oak acorns and bear corn, everything would be alright.

"We need to get going," said Hawk, looking skyward with one wing outstretched toward the tunnel. Just then he was illuminated by another flash of lightning.

Coyote looked at Bobcat. "You lead us this time, Bobbie," he said, "and I'll take up the rear." Bobcat smiled, thinking that Fox would love this moment. She leaped into the black hole in one graceful movement.

"Snake and Salamander, time to load up," said Opossum.

"Sssssss-certainly," said Snake agreeably, as he slithered back inside the berry-stained pouch. Even though Snake was elderly, he would not pass up the chance for this adventure—and wanted to go wherever his medicinal knowledge could be of help.

"If you will kindly give me a lift into this hole," said Salamander, climbing into Opossum's pouch as she spoke, "I will swim across in the small amount of water that has pooled in the middle. Because I can absorb oxygen through my skin, my system is designed so that I can be underwater for a long time. I would prefer this to the pouch, but no offense, Possum."

Opossum started to correct Salamander about her name, but Hawk gave her a sharp look, and she lumbered up into the black hole, Snake and Salamander in tow, following Bobcat in.

"Woodchuck, you next," Hawk directed.

"No," said Woodchuck sadly. "I have seen enough

excitement for one day. I will stay on the North side where things are familiar."

"Are you ready, Turtle?" asked Raccoon.

"No," said Turtle. "I will not be going either. I am old, I cannot travel fast, and I do not want to be a burden to the rest of you. Plus, I am the wisdom keeper. If something were to happen to me, um, all would be lost."

"I understand, and feel sure we will see you again," said Raccoon, respectfully, and followed Opossum into the opening.

"We are staying with you, Turtle and Woodchuck," said Frog, who was sitting very still beside Owl. "I do not do well with stressful situations, and this trek has many unknowns."

"As much as I love an adventure, I do not like to venture far from where I was born," said Owl, reaching down to put one wing on Frog's back and the other on Turtle's. "My place is here with our community, helping others in our home territory. I will see to it that Frog, Turtle, and Woodchuck get back to their homes. But first, let's get some shelter from the storm under these boulders."

Bear turned to Deer to suggest they go in next, but when he looked at her, he realized something that surprised him. He had been thinking only of himself— and had not considered that she might make a decision different from his.

"I'm not going," she said, quietly, just to him. "My hooves are not designed to walk into these curved black holes, and it's just not right for me to go—not now. But you totally are going and do not even hesitate!"

Deer and Bear put their heads on each other's necks, as they had done to comfort each other when their mothers had died. "I love you, Beast," said Bear. Deer couldn't say anything because she was crying.

With Firefly lighting his way, Bear walked bravely into the tunnel just as the heavy rains began. Coyote leapt in behind them.

"Flying over to meet you on the other side," cried Hawk to Coyote between claps of thunder. "Owl," he called over his shoulder, "I'll be in touch as I can!"

"Goodbye, Beast!" Deer said through her tears. But Bear was already gone.

CHAPTER 6
A Traveler Tells of a Landbridge

Bear was halfway through the black hole when the fear struck him again. He was trudging through water that kept getting deeper. And now there was rumbling overhead, and he knew that those same metal boxes with wheels that had killed his mother were passing right over him. But it was comforting that Firefly was riding on his head lighting his way, making little rhymes and flashing as they went along.

"We've gone half*way*,
I can see *day*.
Don't stop now *Bear*
We're almost *there*!"

And Firefly was right—they could see the rosy light of dawn at the end of the tunnel. It wasn't long before the rumbling was receding, and Bear could make out the silhouettes of his friends in line in front of them. Bobcat was leading, followed by Opossum (who had Snake in her pouch), Raccoon was just in front of Bear, and Coyote was behind him. Hawk would be there to greet them when they emerged. In fact, Bear could hear a squawky, shrieking voice echoing into the black hole even now.

Hawk was checking off the travelers as they leaped out of the tunnel: "Bobcat, Possum, Raccoon . . ."

It was Bear's turn, and he tumbled out of the dark, slippery dungeon, happy to be out in the open again. Everything was shiny wet from the rain, and the sun was just coming up above a steep hill that rose up from the bank of the creek. He looked back toward the black hole's opening and saw a rainbow toward the North. Then it hit him that he had just crossed over to the South without actually crossing the Human Highway!

Bear began to feel better. He stretched his body out long, shook out his coat from head to toe, and began to sniff the air for . . . white oak acorns and bear corn! There was a bunch of his favorite food nearby. He could smell it.

"Bear, Firefly, Coyote . . ." Hawk was saying. "Snake?"

"Yesssssss!" said Snake, as Opossum deposited him on a rock near the creek.

"Salamander?"

There was no answer.

"Where is Salamander?" Hawk asked Opossum.

"Don't look at me," she replied. "She gave us all an explanation of how she could breathe underwater and wanted to swim through."

"Oh no!" growled Bobcat. "The water got a lot higher from the rain. I saw something wash past me. It must have been her!"

Everyone began to scan the area calling out: "Salamander? Salamander?"

"Come on out, *Pseudotriton ruber*," Opossum pleaded, hoping her friend would respond to her scientific name. But still there was no answer.

As they searched, the animals realized that they were all very hungry and very sleepy. Before long, everyone had eaten their fill of blueberries, huckleberries, bear corn, acorns, mushrooms, and many other lush and wonderful things. Raccoon even caught herself a tasty crawfish. And before too much longer, everyone had found his or her own moist, shady spot to fall asleep while they waited for Salamander to show up.

The sun was high in the sky when Bear awoke beside a rock near the creek, nose first. He could smell something fishy, and sweet fragrances from the may apples and trout lilies drifting down from the cove above the creek. There was something else too: a really weird oily musky smell that he had never smelled before in his whole life that seemed to be significant somehow.

Nearby Raccoon was fishing, and Opossum was gathering berries, arranging them in her pouch for taking along on their journey. But where were they going to next? Bear wondered. No one was calling for Salamander any longer. She was either not in the area, or . . . something bad had happened to her.

Bear could hear muffled voices coming from under the rhododendron thicket just up the bank.

"We know the lay of the land West of here," Coyote was saying in a low tone, "but we've newly come to this particular area so aren't really familiar with this landscape."

Hawk replied with a slightly less annoying than usual raspy cry: "I say we follow the creek downstream in case we find Salamander."

Suddenly Bear got a much stronger whiff of that weird oily musky scent. It seemed like there was a mysterious power nearby.

"I smell something," Bear said to no one in particular.

"Me too," said Raccoon from a little ways up the creek.

"I can hear it," said Bobcat in her silky, low voice, sidling up beside Bear.

"I see something moving up on the hill," Hawk screeched.

Then Bear could begin to make out something large and tree-like moving down the hill through the thicket toward their group. He sprang up and looked toward Hawk, who was gliding down to land on his shoulders. Everyone rushed to get behind Bear, in case he could protect them. Everyone, that was, except for Opossum, who suddenly keeled over as if she were dead.

"Who's there?" called Bear, making his voice as low and growly as he could.

"What is your business here?" Hawk cried out, his voice cracking with uncertainty.

Suddenly the air was filled with a high-pitched bugling scream, and then a voice deeper and fuller than any they had ever heard before said, "Be not afraid. I am Elk."

At first it seemed that a tree full of branches was appearing over the bushes and moving toward them. Then a chestnut-brown colored head with a mane and a huge tan-colored body poked through the shrubbery. The branches were on its head, and there was a thick, unnatural ring around its neck. The thing looked like a super large version of Deer. Everyone was so stunned that they had nothing to say. They had never in their lives seen such a gigantic, powerful creature.

"Run!" screamed Hawk, flying up into the trees. Everyone started to scatter. Opossum sat up, dazed.

"No!" shouted a very old and very frail voice from

42

the rocks beside the creek, and a loud rattling sound came from the same direction. "I have heard talesssssss of the Elk."

Snake writhed, slithered, and rattled up the bank and onto a higher rock so he could command everyone's attention, including the newcomer.

"Your race is said to be one of the fiercest and gentlest," he said, speaking directly to Elk. "My ancesssssstors told of a day when Human Beingsssss had cut up the entire land—and all the creatures joined forces to reclaim their territories. The legend sssssays that the Bear and the Deer will lie down together, and then the Elk will return and begin to help reconnect the land."

Everyone held this in for a moment. They all trusted Snake. He was both an elder and a healer—and they believed his words.

"Thank you, Father Snake," said Elk, his deep voice booming. "I just arrived from the East, but many moons ago I came here from far to the West. My kind can travel great distances. But tell me, why are you all lingering here near this culvert? It can be a dangerous place."

Coyote explained: "Bobcat and I have just come from the West, but I'm fairly certain we haven't traveled as far as you have. We found this black hole, what you call 'culver,' and took it across to the North side, where we met this lovely group and several of their friends. They were meeting about trying to find a way to cross the Human

Highway safely, so we led them here. Not all of them felt comfortable getting into the culver—and now we are searching for..."

"I believe he said culver*t*, with a T," said a familiar nerdy voice.

"Salamander!" cried Opossum. "You're alive!"

"Yes, but part of me is missing!" said Salamander, seeming more amused than concerned as she crawled up the bank in her wobbly way, then reached behind her with her tiny hands to show everyone that her tail was now only half as long as before.

"What happened?" asked Hawk.

"Yes, tell us!" cooed Raccoon.

"I was swimming through the culver*t*," Salamander began, glancing at Elk to make sure he knew she had learned the correct term for the black hole, "and suddenly the water started moving really fast. It washed me right through there at tip-top speed. I got spit out on this side, and before I knew it, my bottom third was wedged between two small sharp rocks. The only way to get free was to pull hard and . . . and that's how I lost part of my tail. I had to backtrack a bit from downstream to get back here and find you all again."

"You are very brave, Sister Salamander," Elk said admiringly. "These culverts are indeed dangerous. Some creatures—like me—simply cannot use them. Tell me, do you all know about the landbridge?"

Everyone looked around at each other wide-eyed.

"We don't," said Coyote, edging closer to Bobcat.

"Nor do we," said Hawk. "What is it?"

"The landbridge is a place where the Human Highway was cut through a mountainside. The Humans made two tunnels to take their cars through, leaving the land connected at the top. It's the best place in this gorge to go from North to South and back again safely."

Everyone asked questions at the same time.

"How far away is it?" asked Salamander.

"How did you find it?" asked Raccoon.

"Which direction is it?" asked Hawk.

"How many times have you crossed it?" asked Opossum.

"Would you be able to show us?" asked Coyote.

"What's a car?" asked Bear. But as soon as he asked the question, he knew the answer. He knew that "car" must be the word for the horrible metal boxes traveling fast on wheels—the things that had taken his mother from him when he was so very young.

"For you, Brothers and Sisters, it is about four day's travel from here," said Elk, "and it would be my privilege to show you the way."

Hawk flew up and down a few times, excitedly. "Elk, if you can provide me with directions, I'd like to go and scout the landbridge, then return to our home territory on the North side and tell our friends there about it.

Elk described to Hawk the way to the landbridge, and

everyone listened carefully.

"Look after them, Snake," Hawk said to his elder affectionately.

"I ssssshall," said Snake, who then looked right at Elk. The two seemed to have an unspoken understanding. The huge, majestic beast then stepped toward the rock where Snake was reclining, lowering his mighty head as if in a bow toward the medicine keeper, his antlers coming to rest gently upon the rock. Snake writhed and slithered into Elk's antlers, where he would rest and ride throughout the journey ahead.

"See you soon!" Hawk cried as he ascended and caught a fair morning wind blowing warm out of the South, set a course, and headed East.

CHAPTER 7
New Friends Along the Way

The moon was high in the sky, and Elk was carrying Snake in his antlers and leading Bear, Coyote, Bobcat, Raccoon, and Opossum—who had Salamander in her pouch—through the dense forest on a trail he knew well. Firefly flew some of the time and rode on Bear's head the rest of the time.

Opossum also had a supply of berries in her pouch, which Salamander rationed to the others whenever there was not enough food nearby. They had been traveling since they found Salamander in the late afternoon, and it was now the middle of the night. Everyone was beginning to get tired when they heard a faint weeping, crying, moaning sound just ahead of them.

In the moon's light they could see they were approaching an overhanging rock structure that made a little shelter, a small cave. Two sets of eyes were shining out.

48

"Greetings," said a husky voice as the group got closer.

"Greetings to you, friends," said Elk. "Is that you, Skunk?"

"Yes, indeed," said the voice, which came from a small animal who glowed in the moonlight with white zig-zaggy lines that formed a pattern all over its body, with one big white spot right between its eyes.

Bear thought this was very strange, because the skunks he had known had been striped. This one had spots! He thought immediately of Deer. *Beast*, he said secretly, *I wish you were here to see this!*

"That must be *Spilogale putorius*," Salamander whispered, climbing out of Opossum's pouch and onto the ground.

"I'm here with Weasel," Skunk said, sounding rather distressed. "The tip of his long tail got run over on the Human Highway, and he's in a lot of pain." Weasel moaned as if to demonstrate that this was true.

"*Mustela frenata* I'm guessing," said Salamander, nearly giddy with excitement. What she lacked in a tail, she seemed to need to make up for in scientific knowledge.

"Let me sssssseeeeee," hissed Snake with concern. Elk bent down to allow the old fellow to slither over to the odd couple under the overhang. "Firefly, can you lend me your lantern?"

Firefly nodded:

"My light will guide you without *fail*
As you attend to Weasel's *tail*."

"Ah, we need to find sssssssome herbs," Snake said. "Have you sssssseen any Yarrow, Goldenseal, Yellowroot or Wild Ginger nearby?"

"No, not really," said Skunk with a shrug.

"Let's look," said Raccoon, "Come on, Opossum, you can help." Opossum was eating a berry from her pouch.

"Hey, can we have some of your purple berries?" asked Skunk politely. Weasel moaned again.

"Yes," said Opossum, emptying her pocket for her new friends. "We've been eating them all along our journey. You take all of these, and we'll go gather some medicine for Snake to use on Weasel's tail."

Back on the North side, a very tired but happy Hawk was swooping down by the light of the moon to land on the Piney Knob. Owl was camped out there in a scrubby tree, half asleep but with one eye open in case her comrade might return. Below on the ground, Turtle was waiting too.

"News!" Hawk was squawking. "I've got good news!"

Owl glided to the ground and landed beside Turtle

without making a sound. "What is it?" she asked, eyes wide.

"Yes, tell us, please," said Turtle.

"You won't believe all the things that have happened since this time last night!" Hawk cried. "The black hole is called a culvert, and it does lead to the South! Salamander washed out of it with the heavy rains and was lost for a while, but she showed up with part of her tail missing right after we met Elk!"

"Elk?" Turtle asked in amazement.

"Yes, a very big, brave, yet kind and gentle spirit who joined our group and told us about a landbridge, which I've just seen. It's a ways to the East, but I think those who can travel there will want to see it. It's a safe passage!"

"Well, bless me, the legends are true," said Turtle, slowly shaking her head from side to side. "Growing up, my parents spoke of a time in the future when Human Beings had carved up all the land from East to West and North to South. It was said that all the creatures would then begin to work together to reclaim their homelands." Turtle closed her eyes, as if remembering something from long ago. "The Bear and the Deer would lie down together, the Elk would return, and the land would begin to be reconnected."

The sun was high when Bear awoke in the cave next to Bobcat and Coyote. Even though he had not slept very

51

well, his nose, of course, woke up first. There was a very strong, very wonderful smell on the air that he had smelled before, but it had never been this overwhelming.

The scent was like a kind of promise that gave him a springy energy, and he bounded up, yawned, stretched his body out long, shook out his coat from head to toe, and found a good temporary scratch tree. He didn't really feel like eating. All he wanted to do was find the source of that sweet scent.

"He's better! He's well!" Skunk was running around in the cave, circling Weasel, who was sitting up, bright-eyed and somewhat more bushy-tailed, and no longer moaning, thanks to Snake's treatment.

"How are you feeling?" asked Snake, who was coiled up near the patient, various mixtures and tinctures spread around him on the cave floor where Firefly was also resting.

"I'm feeling really healed," squeaked Weasel, surprised. He inspected his tail as if seeing it for the first time. "I was really out of it, you know, before, but now I feel pretty good. The pain's nearly gone!"

"My tail itself is nearly gone," Salamander piped up, "but it'll grow back."

"I'm glad you are better, Weasel," said Coyote. "Perhaps, with a bit more rest, you will accompany us to the landbridge, then."

Weasel looked at Skunk and both nodded. "Agreed,"

they said in unison.

"I'm going to go in search of some . . . ants," said Bear, distractedly, "while the rest of you . . . rest."

"Very well," said Bobcat with a sly smile, as if she knew a secret.

"Don't go too far, Bear," said Elk. "As long as Weasel is feeling good, we'll move on tonight."

Relieved to have time on his own, Bear followed his nose. He left the area of the cave and headed up a small ridge, going wherever the smell seemed strongest. At the top of the little ridge, he picked up a faint, damp trail through a patch of dense woods. He could tell he was very close to the source of the scent when something large and the color of a delicious brown acorn—and similarly shaped—darted out into the trail up ahead. He only saw it for an instant, but it was the most beautiful creature he had ever seen in his whole life. Then, just as quickly as it had come, the coppery form disappeared into the trees.

"Wait!" Bear called. It was like he was in a dream, not fully aware of his actions. Had he just imagined this angelic spirit? Now he was running fast, tumbling after the tawny stranger into the dark woods.

"Wait!" he heard himself saying again to whatever it was. "I haven't eaten a bite or slept for three days and nights. I've been following your scent, and that's how I got here from the other side of the gorge!"

There was a rustling sound, and then he saw a pair of gorgeous big brown eyes peering out from behind a bunch of pipevine.

"You're from the North?" a shy voice asked, very close to him now.

"Yes, indeed," said Bear, his own voice trembling with an excitement he had never known before.

"I'm SheBear," the timid voice cooed as the creature stepped out cautiously from behind the pipevine, knocking off several juicy swallowtail caterpillars in the process. "I've never met anybody from the North before."

Now Bear could see this magnificent being clearly for the first time. She looked just like a slightly smaller version of Bear himself, but she seemed stronger somehow, more muscular, and her coat was not black like his, but shone like the color of cinnamon in the patches of sunlight scattered on the trail. He noticed she was looking him up and down as well.

As if she might disapprove of what she saw, SheBear turned and began to saunter up the trail away from him. Not sure whether or not she wanted him to, Bear followed her closely, putting his own big furry feet into each slightly smaller footprint she made in the moist path. He was relieved when SheBear glanced over her shoulder to make sure her new friend was following.

"Well," said Bear, finally recovering some of his confidence, "I'm called Bear, and I've never met anyone from the South before—that is, except for Bobcat, Coyote, Elk, Skunk, and Weasel. I mean, never anywhere have I ever met anyone as strong and as awesome as you!"

"Aw, Bear! Thank you," said SheBear, turning to bat her unusually round and enchanting eyes, which made Bear feel unbearably weak in his knees. "Where are y'all headed?"

"To a landbridge that Elk knows about," he answered.

SheBear turned around to face him fully. When their eyes met, he knew this was why he had traveled so far.

"You're so beautiful and, so strong and, well, so . . . cinnamon," said Bear nervously.

"And you're so shiny and sable," she said, "with that adorable white bib!"

"Do you want to come with us?" asked Bear.

"Why, sure!" said SheBear, motioning with her auburn head to indicate that Bear should turn and go in the direction from which he had come. "All my life I've wanted to travel. If you promise to let me lead sometimes, I'll follow wherever you go!"

Bear promised.

CHAPTER 8
Reunion on the Landbridge

"How long is it?" asked Salamander.

"You mean the landbridge?" asked Elk.

"I think she means the way *to* the landbridge," said Opossum, who was getting rather weary of carrying Salamander, but didn't want to risk losing the little red genius again.

"It's not much farther now," said Elk reassuringly. "If we keep moving, we should be there before the set of the sun."

After several days and nights of travel, they were stopping at the river for the last time before reaching their destination. Everyone lined up to take a drink: Bobcat, Coyote, Bear, SheBear, Elk with Snake in his antlers, Raccoon with Firefly riding on her head, Salamander, Opossum, Weasel, and Skunk.

"Look!" hissed Bobcat to Coyote.

"I see it," he answered her in a hushed voice.

Upstream just a little ways was the unmistakable black nose, white snout, and red face of a small fox who was also having a drink.

"You talk to it, Bobbie," said Coyote softly. "I don't want to scare it."

"Fox?" Bobcat called out shyly in her low, silky voice.

The little head turned toward them—and froze in place.

"It's okay! We're friends," Bobcat called, taking a step toward the small ginger-haired figure.

"Hi," said the little stranger. She cocked her head to one side, as if trying to solve a riddle. "Do I know you?"

"I'm Bobcat, and this is Coyote. We—"

"You knew my dad!" yipped the new little Fox in a tiny, young voice. "He told us kits about you in the den. He said if anything ever happened to him, you would teach me all his ways. I've just gotten big enough to leave home, and I've been hoping to find you."

Bobcat and Coyote looked at each other, eyes wide. They were speechless.

"That's *Vulpes vulpes*," Salamander said under her breath, but a little too loudly. Opossum raised her snout toward the sky, and Raccoon dropped the crawfish she had just caught.

"Come on down here and let ussssss get a good look

at you," Snake called.

Fox padded down along the edge of the stream to where Coyote and Bobcat were standing. They all sniffed each other politely.

"Welcome, Fox," said Bobcat. How many times had she wanted to be with her old friend again, and now here was his offspring—the next best thing! Bobcat noticed a strange rumbling, vibrating sound coming from deep inside her and welling up and out of her throat, a murmuring pattern that changed with her breath. She was purring!

"Yes, welcome to our band of travelers," barked Coyote, showing a toothy grin. "You look just like your dad—only prettier, of course."

Fox smiled and hung her head, suddenly shy.

"I'm Bear, and this is my girlfriend, SheBear," Bear said proudly. Everyone else began to introduce themselves and make Fox feel comfortable.

"It's time to make the climb," said Elk, "to the landbridge. Young Fox, your home is now behind you. The world is ahead."

After bounding across this boulder-strewn section of the river, up, up, up went the animals, following Elk along a high ridge trail that wound around through ancient tall pines and oaks. Bear could hear the Human Highway far down below. It sounded almost like it was right under them. Out in the West, the sun was getting lower, and they could hear the Thrushes fluting their final songs of the day.

"Are we on it?" asked Bear.

"Yes, we are on it," answered Elk.

"This is all very sssssssssurreal," hissed Snake. "I thought it would be more, well, you know, more dramatic somehow."

"I know what you mean," said Bear. "It doesn't seem like that big of a deal. Like it's been here forever, but we just didn't know."

They emerged into a clearing where they could look down and see that they were right over top of the metal boxes with wheels—the cars that Elk had spoken of and the much bigger ones.

"What are the big ones?" asked Salamander, as if she could read Bear's mind.

"Trucks," said Elk sadly in his lowest voice. He stopped to nibble on some fresh green shoots.

Suddenly they heard wings flapping and a cry pierced the air.

"Make way!" shrieked a familiar voice. Then there was a tremendous rush of wind as Hawk fluttered in for a landing, followed by the silent swooping figure of Owl!

Bear was so happy. How wonderful it was to see his

old friends! Hawk must have talked Owl into flying up here to see the landbridge.

"Here! Here!" Hawk was squawking over his shoulder. "They're up here!"

Hawk and Owl each spread their right wings as if to reach out to someone, and as they stepped back, Bear couldn't believe his eyes. There was Deer!

"Beast!" Bear huffed.

"Beast!" Deer bleated with joy.

"I've never been happier to see anyone in my whole life," Bear said. "Well, almost never," he corrected himself, glancing at SheBear beside him.

Deer smiled and looked behind her, motioning with a turn of her neck to someone else. Up came a teeny tiny little deer with white spots all over. Then another one joined it. Twin fawns!

"Beast," said Bear, "you've been busy! Now I see why you didn't want to go into the black hole."

"Yes, they came the night you left. And, it looks like you have found your soul mate, after all," Deer said, looking approvingly at SheBear.

"Is that who I think it is?" asked Snake from his spot in Elk's antlers. "I think I'm going to need to get down."

Frog was hopping toward the group, moving as fast as he could to reach the reunion. "Hey folks," he called out cheerfully. Elk set Snake upon the cool ground, and he writhed and slithered towards his buddy.

Raccoon and Opossum ran to see Woodchuck, who had just arrived with a new Squirrel friend.

"Good to see you Possum," Woodchuck teased. "Salamander, we heard you lost your tail."

"Look, it's coming back!" Salamander replied, showing off her already partially regrown tail.

"You know it's Opossum, Woodchuck!" Opossum was saying, but she wasn't really too upset.

Firefly was flashing, Frog was hopping, and Raccoon was handing out berries and other snacks. Snake was so excited he was rattling as he slithered around to gather herbs and mushrooms for the celebration, which Opossum helped him prepare. Bear was introducing the others to SheBear, Weasel, Skunk, and Fox when Salamander suddenly yelled out: *Terrapene carolina!*

They all turned to see their elder, Turtle, the wisdom keeper, slowly making her way toward them.

"I'm... um... just... *barely*... here," she said in a weak, gurgley voice. "But I... just... couldn't... miss this."

Snake rushed over to greet Turtle. "You remember the legends of the Elk's return, right Turtle?"

"Indeed," Turtle said, catching her breath. "Elk, tell us... where you come from and... what you have seen."

As the sun began to set far to the West over the Human Highway, everyone settled into a circle around Elk. Bear lay down on his back with SheBear on one side and Deer and her fawns on the other. The young Fox was sitting between Coyote and Bobcat, who just couldn't seem to stop purring. Everyone munched on mushrooms, herbs, and berries as Elk began to tell how he had come long ago from the West, and that he had crossed more Human Highways than any of them could possibly imagine.

"I've seen things you creatures would not believe," he said. "We animals need to travel in order to find food, attract mates, and help our kind live strong into the future. But our lands truly are completely carved up into tiny pieces by all these roads."

"But why?" asked Woodchuck.

"Because Human Beings want to travel, too," Elk replied. "Brothers and Sisters, when they made this Human Highway, they were not thinking of us. This landbridge we are standing on is a result of the Human Beings making two tunnels for their cars and trucks to pass through the mountain. They didn't really know it, but they were helping us by leaving a bit of our land connected on top."

"Why aren't there more places like this?" asked Coyote.

"By the time this young fox and these baby fawns are grown up, I think there will be," answered Elk. "Right now, all over the land, animals just like you are deciding that they simply cannot try to cross any more. They are abandoning ancient trails and changing their home territories like you have. The Human Highway has become a barrier."

"A sad but necessary consequence of Turtle's Law," said Turtle.

"And why we formed the Forest Council," said Owl.

"And why even though naturally many of us would not get along," said Frog, "we've all been working together as a team to find a solution."

"Exactly," said Elk. "All over the land, animals like you are helping each other to try to find safe passages. But let me tell you something that will really shock you."

"What?" said Bear, putting his head on SheBear's shoulder.

"Tell us," said Deer, nuzzling her fawns.

"In many places, all over the land, to the North, South, East, and West," Elk continued, "some special Human Beings are also working together to find solutions—for us. Some of them are trying to think like we think. Some are watching us carefully to figure out where we try to cross. Some are closing roads during the times we need to move the most. And some are even building landbridges to go over the roads and raising up Human Highways so we can go underneath."

"You mean you can raise up a Human Highway?" asked Bobcat.

"Indeed," nodded Elk. "Sometimes that is even easier than building black holes underneath."

"Is the thing you carry around your neck how the

Human Beings are watching you?" asked Owl.

"Yes," said Elk. "But you all must trust me on this—it is a good thing. I have been traveling very long distances because of the lack of crossings close to where I once lived in the West. Great numbers of my kind are getting killed. We need to be able to cross in many areas in order to prosper and grow our herd. At first my collar was hard to accept. But I got used to it. It is a way I can help all elk—and all of you."

"A collar to save all *Cervus canadensis*," said Salamander, approvingly.

"Indeed," Elk agreed.

"Will there be ways for the smaller ones of us to cross too?" asked Frog.

"Yes," said Elk. "I've seen Human Beings carrying frogs, snakes, turtles, and even salamanders to keep them safe until special ways for them to cross can be built."

Everyone gazed West to where the last light of the setting sun was fading. The Thrushes had gone to bed, and a Whippoorwill began to sing. It was the gloaming, the magical hour, and Firefly flashed out a new poem:

"Keep us all *alive*
Safe passage, free and *easy*
Let our kind *thrive*
The way it's supposed to *be*

Of thee our new land*bridge*
It's time to *sing*
From every mountain *ridge*
Let freedom *ring*"

Elk then let out the same otherworldly, high-pitched bugling scream as he had when they saw him for the first time. It echoed down over the Human Highway.

"What we have got to do now," Elk's deep voice bellowed out, "is communicate to the Human Beings about what we need. Before long, more and more of them will begin to understand how important it is that we be able to cross, and they will figure out how to make more safe passages."

"That will be long after my time," said Snake.

"And mine," said Turtle. "But once . . . *we* were here."

MEET THE REAL ANIMALS

The animals in this story are all species that live in Southern Appalachia. Many of them also are found in other regions of the United States and North America, and even on other continents.

Although the story is fiction, it is based on a real situation and set in a real place: The Pigeon River Gorge in East Tennessee and Western North Carolina near the border of Great Smoky Mountains National Park. Cutting through this beautiful landscape is Interstate 40. Along a curvy 28-mile stretch of this busy highway, many animals are killed by cars and trucks every year.

Read on to learn more about how these species are affected by roads. Each species is listed with its common name, scientific name, and front and back track (if it has one).

A WORD ABOUT ANTHROPOMORPHISM

When we describe animals in a way that gives them human characteristics (like talking) or emotions (like feeling sad), it is called *anthropomorphism*. While doing this helps us understand issues such as the need for better ways to cross roads, scientists work hard not to anthropomorphize in their work because this can interfere with a broad understanding of animal behavior.

AMERICAN BLACK BEAR
Ursus americanus

Black bears are strong, smart, and, like Bear in our story, love their favorite scratch trees, white oak acorns, and bear corn. They also enjoy flipping over rocks and tearing into rotting logs in search of insects and other small animals. Great Smoky Mountains National Park is the largest protected black bear habitat in the eastern US, with approximately 1,900 bears. Not all are black; they can also be white, blonde, brown, or cinnamon, like the character SheBear. Although in our story Bear and Deer are best friends, in real life, an adult bear might eat a baby deer. While a mother bear can scale the tall barriers that divide many highways, her cubs may not be able to get a grip on the slick concrete. Both mother and cubs often get hit as they try to solve the problem.

WHITE-TAILED DEER
Odocoileus virginianus

Deer are common on many continents. White-tailed deer thrive when forests are converted to farmland. Mother deer leave their fawns alone for several hours at a time while foraging for food. The fawns lie still, their spotted coats providing the perfect camouflage. The young have almost no scent, so predators such as bear, coyote, fox, and bobcat will likely not detect them. It is unlikely that tiny fawns like the ones in our story could actually travel as far as they did just after being born. Because there are so many deer moving on the landscape, they are the large animal we most commonly see hit and killed crossing highways. Like other large mammals, they can't always see over tall highway median barriers, so they may successfully cross one side of the highway but not the other.

WOODCHUCK
Marmota monax

Also known as groundhogs, woodchucks can often be seen grazing very close to busy roadways, sometimes standing up on their hind legs, seemingly unruffled by the noise and speed of traffic. This is simply because some of the best food grows close to the roadway, made extra juicy from water running off the concrete and into the side of the road. Often these daredevil antics cost them their lives. Woodchucks form extensive underground burrow systems. When hibernating, their body temperature can reach as low as 36 degrees and their breathing slows to one breath every few minutes. Also called whistle pigs, groundhogs are related to western marmots and prairie dogs, and although more solitary in comparison share a similar predator warning system with their whistling.

EASTERN GRAY SQUIRREL
Sciurus carolinensis

Eastern gray squirrels are found in wooded areas with many types of trees that provide the nuts they crave. They make two types of nests: traditional cavity nests and leaf nests, which are built by young squirrels such as the ones in our story. When it comes to crossing roads, squirrels can make jerky movements and suddenly change direction as if not being able to decide which way to go. This often leads to them getting hit and killed and may be why, if we cannot depend on someone, we say that person is "squirrely." Gray squirrels are an abundant food source within the forest ecosystem for many species, including those in the story: coyote, red fox, red-tailed hawk, and bobcat.

RED-TAILED HAWK
Buteo jamaicensis

The red-tailed hawk is one of the largest members of the hawk family. Adults can have a wingspan of nearly five feet. Hawk in our story spends time above the highway to report the traffic and weather, but the real-life hawks circling high above the roadway are looking for prey such as squirrels and snakes. They soar especially high in the late afternoon, taking advantage of thermals rising from the sun-warmed land below. They emit a hoarse, descending scream-like *kee-eeeee-arr*. Even though they can fly, hawks that swoop into traffic to snatch a meal can be killed in an instant. If you look up next time you see a red-tailed hawk above the road, watch for their red tail feathers shining in the sun.

75

COYOTE
Canis latrans

In the past coyotes normally lived in the more arid, open western two-thirds of North America. Human activities like forest clearing and removal of predators and competitors (like the eastern cougar and the gray wolf and red wolf) gave coyotes a chance to expand their natural range. Coyotes are opportunistic feeders and have an amazingly diverse diet that includes rodents, rabbits, deer, birds, frogs, snakes, carrion, insects, fruits and berries, and grasses. Unlike Coyote in our story, real-life coyotes would be unlikely to team up with a bobcat or fox. But footage showing that coyotes and badgers do travel and hunt together was one of many inspirations for this book.

BOBCAT
Lynx rufus

The bobcat can be identified by its "bobbed" tail that is only about six inches long and tipped with black. The underside of the tail is bright white, and when raised, signals to the female bobcat's kittens that it is safe to move about the forest. While it may look like a cute housecat with its tufted ears and white underbelly, a full-grown adult bobcat weighs in at 30 pounds and will catch prey up to three times its own weight but prefers rabbits and hares. In addition to hissing, growling, and emitting a sound that some compare to the cry of a human baby, bobcats do actually purr, just like Bobcat in our story. A bobcat who passed in front of the author's car inspired the Bobbie character in this book.

RED FOX
Vulpes vulpes

The red fox is the largest member of the fox family and
can be found across North America, Europe, Asia, and
parts of Africa. They are also hit and killed on roads on all
of these continents. Like coyotes, they dig underground
dens to birth and raise their young pups. Although this
species is known for its bright red fur, the pups are brown
or grey when born but change to red within a month.
Foxes generally run in pairs or with a family group. They
have long played important roles in human folklore and
mythology. Red foxes dine mostly on small rodents but
will also eat berries, insects, and birds, as well as raccoons,
squirrels, and opossums, among many other species. They
have impressive hearing and can locate rodents digging
several inches underground.

BARRED OWL
Strix varia

Sometimes called the "hoot owl," the barred owl is named for the bars or dusky markings on its underside. It has a wingspan of up to four feet and is nocturnal, which means it is mostly active at night, when it can be struck by a vehicle while swooping down to catch prey. Their diet mainly consists of small rodents, but they will also eat birds, reptiles, amphibians, and just about any small animal they can catch. Their call is loud and can be heard up to half a mile away. There is a common "mnemonic" (way to remember) for the barred owl's call: "Who cooks for you? Who cooks for you all?" Whereas red-tailed hawks prefer open woods, edges, and fields, barred owls like deeper forests and coves. They raise their small brood in a nest in a tree hollow or snag.

TIMBER RATTLESNAKE
Crotalus horridus

Slow-moving, docile, and shy, timber rattlesnakes are pit vipers, which means they have heat-detecting pits on their faces that enable them to track warm-blooded prey, mostly rodents. By eating large numbers of small mammals, they indirectly consume thousands of Lyme disease-carrying ticks each year. Young rattlers may be eaten by coyotes, bobcats, foxes, skunks, and hawks. Snakes relish the stored-heat energy of rocks and roads, which can spell disaster when vehicles approach more quickly than the snake can slither out of the way. They can live up to 30 years. Females give live birth (eggs hatch internally) to an average of 6–8 young every 2–5 years. Due to habitat destruction and purposeful and accidental killing, they are declining throughout much of Southern Appalachia.

COMMON EASTERN FIREFLY
Photinus pyralis

While Firefly is the smallest character in this book, he represents a large family of light-producing beetles as there are more than 9,000 known species of firefly around the world. In North America, the one you are most likely to see is common eastern firefly, which is also called the "big dipper" for the J-shaped flying and flashing pattern the males use to attract females. Fireflies cannot survive when their habitat is destroyed—such as when roads are built on top of their mating grounds. It's no coincidence that Firefly in our story speaks in rhyme because fireflies often flash with a rhythm and sequence that is not unlike poetry. Because they communicate in flashes of light, human light pollution can affect their ability to locate each other and find mates.

WOOD FROG
Lithobates sylvaticus

Frogs are fragile so changes in the environment can create stress for them. Wood frogs belong to the Ranid group of frogs that have large, strong hind legs for jumping and are capable of traveling a mile or more to summer breeding ponds and over-wintering habitats. The wood frog has adapted to tolerate freezing over much of its body during winters, when it deposits eggs in seasonal pools. Although some frogs remain fairly close to where they were born, wood frogs move out into different areas of the forest. This keeps their genes strong and diverse, but it can also put them in danger if roads are between them their desired new home. In some places in the US, groups of concerned citizens carry frogs across roads when they need to travel in great numbers to breed.

VIRGINIA OPOSSUM
Didelphis virginiana

Female Virginia opossums do have a pouch like our story's Opossum, though it's used not to tote berries but to carry offspring. This qualifies them as North America's only marsupial. As the young age they leave the pouch, climb onto their mother's back, and cling to her while she hunts. The opossum's tail is adapted for grasping so it can carry leaves and twigs to line its burrows. Slow moving, short sighted, and likely to freeze in the face of danger, opossums are frequently killed on roads. Like the timber rattlesnake, one opossum can devour more than 4,000 ticks in a season, an important contribution toward controlling Lyme disease. Opossum wants her name pronounced with the O because "Possum" with a P refers to a different marsupial in Australia.

RACCOON
Procyon lotor

Raccoons are a common and crafty resident of Southern Appalachian forests—and have secured a solid place in most urban settings as well. These masked and ring-tailed mammals are omnivores, eating everything they find on their nocturnal forages, from crayfish to blueberries. Just like Raccoon in our story, real raccoons can be seen washing their food in streams with their dexterous front paws. While captive individuals can live up to 20 years, raccoons in the wild rarely survive past three years of age, and vehicle injury is a major cause of their short life expectancy. Raccoons, with their exceptional night vision and climbing ability and agility, are capable of using a variety of structures, when available, to safely cross the highway.

RED SALAMANDER
Pseudotriton ruber

This bright red-to-orange salamander is "endemic" or restricted to the eastern United States, where it is common but threatened by loss of its habitat. It is considered semi-aquatic and so is most successful in forested areas that have rivers, streams, and creeks. Red salamanders stay in springs or streams during the winter, traveling over land during the other seasons. They are most active at night, and large groups of them can be seen crossing roads together at certain times, which has led to concerned citizens stopping traffic to help them cross safely. They can indeed regenerate lost or injured limbs or tails like our story's nerdy Salamander, though the process takes several weeks. It is unlikely any red salamanders have hitched a ride in an opossum's pouch.

EASTERN BOX TURTLE
Terrapene carolina carolina

The eastern box turtle can retract into its shell and close itself off from predators. Damaged shells can regenerate and reform. Males have reddish eyes, while the females' eyes are brown. Box turtles can live up to 100 years so long as they don't get caught in a roadway when traffic is coming. Some individuals, like Turtle in our story, have been around since before roads infringed upon their ancient trails, so it's easy to understand why these slow-moving creatures attempt often-futile crossings. They are especially active on our roadways during spring and fall due to more moderate temperatures compared to summer and winter. Females build their underground nests with their hind legs and lay on average 3–5 eggs that typically hatch in mid-summer to early fall.

ELK
Cervus canadensis

Elk range in woods, meadows, and forest edges, eating plants, leaves, and grasses. During the fall rut, males make impressive bugling calls to establish dominance and attract females. This large member of the deer family was successfully reintroduced to Great Smoky Mountains National Park in 2001. The original herd has now splintered to areas outside the park boundary. As elk continue to move out of the park, more are hit and killed on roadways in East Tennessee and Western North Carolina. Some are badly injured and have to suffer until they die unless wildlife biologists can find them and put them out of their misery. Because a mature bull elk can weigh more than 700 pounds, a vehicle collision with an elk is definitely a safety hazard for humans.

EASTERN SPOTTED SKUNK
Spilogale putorius

This small skunk species has a distinctive black-and-white spotted pattern. It is slender and more weasel-like in body shape than the more common striped skunk. Though both species are famous for their unpleasant scent—released as a spray only when they are threatened or provoked—spotted skunks are also known for a defensive handstand behavior they use to intimidate predators. Conservation groups in Southern Appalachia are working to save the spotted skunk from endangerment due to habitat loss and fragmentation. Unlike striped skunks, they are tree climbers. Researchers have found this elusive and increasingly rare species in the Pigeon River Gorge. Because they prefer shrubby and rocky closed habitats, the openness of highways can serve as a barrier to their movement.

LONG-TAILED WEASEL
Mustela frenata

The long-tailed weasel has a small head with long whiskers and black eyes. In colder climates, their winter coats are white, but in Southern Appalachia, they are a buff color. This weasel's scent glands produce a musky odor which, instead of spraying like a skunk, they leave behind through a process of dragging and rubbing over surfaces. Due to their high metabolism, they must eat often and therefore are constantly on the move, sometimes traveling miles in one day in search of food (and mates too). Because they are secretive and hard to see, we don't know how many there are. Researchers have observed several in the Pigeon River Gorge and are beginning to study them. If built correctly, small dark culverts may successfully help these weasels cross under the highway.

PHOTO CREDITS

Black bear and elk - Joye Ardyn Durham
White-tailed deer - Henry Weinberg
Groundhog - Tim Parker
Red-tailed hawk - Karen Wilkinson
Coyote - Connar L'Ecuyer
Bobcat - Marshal Hedin
Red fox - Emmanuel Keller
Barred owl - GoldenBright Photography
Timber rattlesnake - Peter Paplanus
Common eastern firefly - Terry Priest
Wood frog - Warren Lynn
Virginia opposum - Richard Coldiron
Raccoon - Krystal Hamlin
Black-chinned red salamander - Ashley Wahlberg
Eastern box turtle - Great Smoky Mountains Association
Eastern spotted skunk - National Park Service
Long-tailed weasel - Matt Lavin

ADDITIONAL READING

Birds of the Smokies by Fred J. Alsop III

Firefly Experience by Radim Schreiber

Frequently Asked Questions About Smoky Mountain Black Bears by Courtney Lix

Living with Bears Handbook by Linda Masterson, 2nd ed.

Mammals of the Smokies by Edward Pivorun

Mountain Nature: A Seasonal Natural History of the Southern Appalachians by Jennifer Frick-Ruppert

Reptiles and Amphibians of the Smokies by Stephen G. Tilley and James E. Huheey

Scats and Tracks of the Southeast by James C. Halfpenny and Jim Bruchac

Smoky Mountain Elk: Return of the Native by Rose Houk

Especially for educators

Safe Passage Discussion Questions for Teachers are available at SmokiesInformation.org and SmokiesSafePassage.org or by emailing frances@gsmassoc.org.

HOW TO HELP THEM CROSS

Long before humans ever thought about building roads for their own travel, animals had created ancient trails, often near sources of water. They followed these trails by instinct across the land to get many things they needed to be successful in life, or to *thrive*. Food, shelter, and mates were high on the animals' list of needs.

Now, our roads crisscross those same ancient trails in every part of the world. But wild animals still try to use their old routes because they still need to get a variety of foods and find healthy mates outside their own families.

The more vehicles traveling on roads, the harder it is for wildlife to cross successfully. As long as animals keep trying to cross, humans can also be injured or killed in the accidents or *collisions* that result.

To make roads safer for both wildlife and people, a group near Great Smoky Mountains National Park is working to make changes to highways. Learn about Safe Passage: The Pigeon River Gorge Wildlife Crossing Project at SmokiesSafePassage.org.

TURTLE'S LAW = THE BARRIER EFFECT

In our story, the elder of the Forest Council, Turtle, creates a law to keep the animals safe: She forbids them even to try to cross the Human Highway. This illustrates what scientists call the *barrier effect*.

When any type of animal finally stops trying to cross, the highway has become a *barrier*, and some species will be at risk of dying out—becoming *extinct*. This is because where the animals live (their *habitat*) is now broken into pieces (called *fragments*) and so they can no longer breed in a healthy way.

It is up to humans to help animals cross our roads, or else we may lose some of them forever.

Each time animals like this coyote in Shenandoah National Park decide to cross a road, they risk their lives. When wildlife choose to no longer take that risk, the road becomes a barrier. Photo by B. Kuhns

THE IMPORTANCE OF SPECIES DIVERSITY

Why is the loss of a single animal species important? Even the smallest species is part of the natural balance that keeps all of us alive. This balance is known as *species diversity*.

John Muir, who was one of the first to work hard to protect animals' homelands from being destroyed, said, "When we try to pick out anything by itself, we find it

Spotted salamanders are both predators of insects and prey for larger carnivores. They often cross roads in spring while looking for ponds to lay their eggs in. Photo by Adam Cushen

hitched to everything else in the universe." In other words, if something we do affects one type of animal, it can also affect many others, including humans.

The famous scientist and author E. O. Wilson pointed out that, "if insects were to vanish, the environment would collapse into chaos."

So, for all of us to thrive and be whole as a planet, we need to think about the needs of every type of creature, large and small alike.

ROAD ECOLOGY AND WILDLIFE CROSSING STRUCTURES

For years, people around the world have been working to make roads safer for both animals and humans. They study and practice what is known as *road ecology.*

"The solution to addressing issues of wildlife and highway interaction is two-pronged: fencing plus crossing structures," says Terry McGuire, a retired highway engineer with Parks Canada and a road ecology expert. "It has been shown through research that one does not work as effectively without the other."

While some animals take years to become comfortable using crossing structures, others can adapt to them quite quickly. Fencing guides wildlife to crossing opportunities, saving individual lives and helping populations thrive.

Fencing and crossing structures have been used successfully all over the world, from France and Germany to Singapore and South Korea. Our North American neighbors Canada and Mexico have also created effective crossings. Now US states like California, Washington, Utah, Texas, North Carolina, and Tennessee are focusing on road ecology too.

In the Southern Appalachians, black bear, elk, and white-tailed deer are the biggest animals that get hit on roads. They are called *megafauna.* While you might survive if your family's vehicle hit a deer or even a bear, running into a huge elk can kill you. If your family car collides with these animals, it can cost a lot to get the vehicle fixed.

Most wildlife crossings focus on megafauna with little emphasis on smaller species since the feeling is that they do not create a safety threat to vehicles. But, in the grand scheme, it is just as important for the smaller species to cross roads so that they, too, can continue to thrive.

To make roads safer for both wildlife and people, a group near Great Smoky Mountains National Park is working to make changes to highways. Learn about Safe Passage: The Pigeon River Gorge Wildlife Crossing Project at SmokiesSafePassage.org.

PLANNING AND TYPES OF WILDLIFE CROSSINGS

It is important to locate wildlife crossings where animals wish to cross the road, not just where it may be easy or convenient from a construction perspective. Scientists

and researchers help road planners know where animals try to cross by studying *wildlife mortality, collision data, migration routes,* and the *geographical terrain* of the area.

One type of crossing does not necessarily meet every animal's needs and, ideally, a combination of various crossing types (like

Strategic use of fencing and escape ramps (like this one) can help wildlife navigate the landscape surrounding the crossing. Photo courtesy of Colorado Dept. of Transportation a buffet of choices) should be provided, spaced out in such a way that animals do not need to travel great distances to find a crossing.

Most wildlife shy away from anything that looks like a trap, and so at first animals may not want to use wildlife crossing structures. How an animal gets to the crossing structure is called the *approach*. Having trees and plants (*vegetation*) close to the structure reduces light and noise and gives animals protective cover. Fencing must be put in place to direct them to a new crossing structure, or they may choose to cross the highway rather than use something unknown. Sometimes an animal trying to use a structure will find itself in the road, and so an escape ramp must be close by so it will not be trapped. All of these aspects need to be considered as part of the planning process if a wildlife crossing structure is to be successful.

A female elk (cow) stands beside a road sign near Cherokee. North Carolina. Photo by Doris Boteler

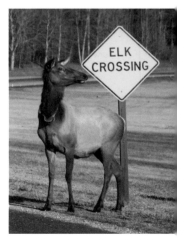

Signs: Old-fashioned road signs don't cost much to put up and can help make drivers aware an animal may be crossing and remind them to go slower for safety. They work best in parks where speed limits are already low, but still they cannot save animals' lives or prevent collisions.

Interactive signs notify drivers when animals are active in or near the roadway. Photo courtesy of Colorado Dept. of Transportation

A bobcat utilizes a round culvert to navigate under Interstate 40 in Tennessee. Photo courtesy of National Parks Conservation Association and Wildlands Network

Interactive Signs: These are electric signs that turn on when an animal is crossing or starting to come into the road. They can help by getting drivers to slow down and watch for wildlife. They are a bit more expensive than basic signs, work best on small roads without much traffic, and can only detect large animals.

Round Culverts: Made of metal, cement, or plastic, culverts may be round or elliptical in shape and cost less than many other types of crossing structures. They are used well by many small species to pass under the highway. Coyotes and bobcats like them too, but larger species usually reject them because they are so dark and may seem like a trap.

Box Culverts: Offering more space and better footing than round culverts, box culverts come in many sizes and can save the lives of small, medium, and large animals. In the southwestern US they channel water from flash floods and allow many species to cross under roads as well. They have been shown to work for bear, deer, and many other small- to medium-sized mammals for a modest cost. These types of structures can also be designed to aid crossing for reptiles and amphibians.

Multi-Plate Arches: These are made of curved steel plates that are usually brought to the road and put together there. They can often work just as well as more expensive structures for megafauna such as bear, deer, and elk—and for mountain lions in the west. As with culverts, some animal species might refuse to go into a multi-plate arch because of the lack of natural light and feeling of being confined or fear of being trapped.

Large mammals like black bears may be more inclined to use a box culvert than a round one. Photo courtesy of Montana Department of Transportation, Confederated Salish and Kootenai Tribes, and Western Transportation Institute– Montana State University

This multi-plate arch in Montana offers a spacious underpass for a modest cost. Photo by Marcel Huijser

99

The passages under open-span bridges like this one in Colorado are widely used by many species. Photo by Julia Kintsch

Open-Span Bridges: In places where it is critically important to connect wildlife habitat, such as migration routes, open-span bridges are highly recommended. A more expensive option than culverts or arches, these bridges can cost more than one million dollars each. In the western states and Canada, they have been seen to work well for large wildlife including bear, deer, elk, mountain lions, and wolves—and to help smaller species as well.

A young mule deer investigates a wildlife monitoring camera under a bridge extension on I-90 in Washington State. Photo courtesy of Washington State Dept. of Transportation

Bridge Extensions: When animals travel, they often follow water drainages, so making a bridge extension is one of the most effective ways to help wildlife to cross highways. Animals of all sizes are comfortable passing under bridges because, unlike in a culvert or arch, there is plenty of natural light and they do not feel confined. Bridge extensions can be expensive, but since transportation departments often make road repairs, creating wildlife crossings can become a part of that process, saving animals' lives.

Wildlife Overpasses:

Because they can work well for the most species, wildlife overpasses may be the best solution to wildlife crossing needs. Species like moose and antelope that will not cross underneath the highway can thrive using an overpass. Though this is the most expensive type of wildlife crossing structure, it has been used with great success to save animal lives in Europe

A wildlife overpass on the Trans-Canada highway in Banff National Park. Wildlife overpasses are more expensive than other options, but they offer superior connectivity for wildlife that will not cross under roads. Photo by coolcaesar

and Canada. Overpasses are now being considered in states including Colorado, Washington, and Utah among others.

Source: Bill Ruediger, Wildlife Consulting Resources, *Safe Passage: A User's Guide to Developing Effective Highway Crossings for Carnivores and Other Wildlife*

INFLUENCES, ALLUSIONS, AND THANKS

As a student of English literature, I was fascinated by the use of allusion, how authors wove into a story or poem indirect references to the words of well-known authors who had influenced them. This paid respect to great works of literature while at the same time invoking their power. In writing this book, I found that allusions to my own creative influences seemed to flow naturally from my passion for the topic of saving wildlife.

Where I live, in the region surrounding Great Smoky Mountains National Park, great numbers of black bears are struck and killed each year on our highways. Now the reintroduced elk are also moving out of the park and attempting to cross the roads, joining their cousins, the prolific white-tailed deer, in sad deaths often involving hours of suffering.

For the past several years, I've been part of a group collaborating to make highways safer for both animals and people in East Tennessee and Western North Carolina. In early 2020, just as the COVID-19 pandemic started, a colleague in this work, Taylor Barnhill, challenged me to write a book to teach young people about the need for

The I-40 Pigeon River Gorge Wildlife Crossing Project

wildlife crossings. As I geared up for this undertaking, the voice of one of my favorite singer songwriters, David Crosby, came to mind. His haunting post-apocalyptic anthem "Wooden Ships" became the soundtrack for my creative work on *A Search for Safe Passage*.

In the song, two groups of desolate people from opposite sides of a war encounter each other after the destruction has rendered them weak and nearly dead—and some don't even know who won! The song began to represent for me a dreadful future when we have lost our iconic Appalachian species to our own blindness and apathy—a time when humans would say to the few remaining individual bear, deer, and elk:

Horror grips us as we watch you die
All we can do is echo your anguished cries

And the animals would reply:
We are leaving, you don't need us.

Oh, but we do need them! *A Search for Safe Passage* alludes to "Wooden Ships" in several ways. Since the animal territory in the gorge is now divided by the highway into the North and South, those on the North side believe that the ones in the South have shinier coats because they live nearer to the river. So, Deer says to Bobcat in Chapter 4, "I can see by your coat, my friend, you're from the other side." Later, at the end of Chapter 6, Hawk catches "a fair wind blowing warm out of the South" and "sets a course" like the narrator at the end of "Wooden Ships." Then, in Chapter 7, Skunk asks Opossum a famous question from the song: "Hey, can I have some of your purple berries?" And in Firefly's final poem, the lines "free and easy," and "the way it's supposed to be," also come from "Wooden Ships." Firefly's poem actually satirically combines Crosby's lyrics with some from Samuel Francis Smith's "America (My Country, 'Tis of Thee)." I also allude to the influence of Croz with the moniker "Human Highway," the name of a Crosby, Stills, Nash, and Young album that was never published.

There are also allusions throughout the book to my fellow Kentucky native Tom T. Hall's song "That's How I Got to Memphis."

We all have stories about how we got to where we are, and Memphis in this song is just a metaphor for wherever we find ourselves. When Salamander reappears in Chapter 6 after being lost during the culvert crossing, she says, "and that's how I lost part of my tail." Just as humans often travel because they fall in love and move to where their sweetheart lives, animals travel because they have a strong drive to find the right mate. This is especially reflected in the passage in Chapter 7 where Bear finally meets SheBear, whose scent he has been aware of since he first awakens at the top of Chapter 1. "I haven't eaten a bite or slept for three days and nights" comes from the song; Bear's words, "that's how I got here from the other side of the gorge," allude to it, and the big tip-off is SheBear's final declaration, "I'll follow wherever you go."

There are other allusions—to The Who, to J. R. R. Tolkien's *Lord of the Rings*, to the films of Wes Anderson, and even to the Bible. When Elk tells the group on the landbridge, "I've seen things you creatures would not believe," he is channeling the character Roy Batty from the film *Blade Runner*, based on the book *Do Androids Dream of Electric Sheep?* by Philip K. Dick. This reference suggests a comparison between the *Blade Runner* society's treatment of replicants and how we regard animals.

A Search for Safe Passage also pays cultural homage to the first peoples who lived on our Southern Appalachian land, the Cherokee. Using the simplest of possible names for the animal characters—Bear, Deer, Elk, Coyote, Bobcat and so on—is a nod to native peoples' ancient myths. In Chapter 4, Snake says his kind have nearly been "rubbed out," a term frequently used by the Native Americans in the film *Little Big Man* to refer to their tribes' decimation. Indians in that work—based on the novel of the same name by James Berger—also refer to whites as "Human Beings," as do Raccoon, Turtle, Snake, and Elk in *A Search for Safe Passage*. The last line of the book, "But once . . . we were here," is also the last line of the epic film *Last of the Mohicans* based on the novel by James Fenimore Cooper. It is spoken by the warrior Chingachgook after his son is killed, leaving him the last remaining member of his tribe.

Anyone who shares my appreciation for the Myers–Briggs Type Indicator will likely recognize that the characters each have a specific personality type based on my favorite reference book, *Please Understand Me II* by David Keirsey. Once I assigned them their types, the animals came to life and wrote the story right in front of my eyes. All I had to do was type fast enough to keep up with them.

This book would not have been possible without the natural history mentoring of my husband, John Philip Beaudet; the gracious biological advising of National Parks Conservation Association Volgenau Fellow Steve Goodman; the dignified and anatomically true renderings of my cast by Great Smoky Mountains Association Publications Specialist Emma DuFort; and the direction and wisdom of National Parks Conservation Association's Senior Program Manager Jeffrey Hunter, facilitator for Safe Passage: The Pigeon River Gorge Wildlife Crossing Project. Each offered their gifts to the making of this book in their own inimitable way, for which I am deeply grateful.

Final recognition goes to another musician, singer–songwriter Jonathan Byrd of Mebane, North Carolina, who coached me as I wrote a folk song to support this book and wildlife crossing projects everywhere. The lyrics to "Safe Passage: Animals Need a Hand" are included here and, thanks to Anne C. May of Great Smoky Mountains Association, the sheet music can help musicians sing and play it. Look for the song on YouTube and at SmokiesSafePassage.org.

~Frances Figart (frances@gsmassoc.org)

SAFE PASSAGE: ANIMALS NEED A HAND

Frances Figart

I am an A - mer - i - can Black Bear and I'm fol - low - ing an an - cient trail.

Drum   Drum   Drum   Drum (continue throughout...)

I am a Bear.   By the side of the road I   wait   to

fol - low the an - cient   trail   cut   through by the in - ter - state.

Safe   pas - sage: An - i - mals need a   hand.   Let's

change our roads to help them cross and move on o - ver this land.

Drum   Drum   Drum   Drum

I am a Deer and I die ev - er - y day

fol - low - ing the an - cient trail on to the hu - man high - way.

Safe pas - sage: An - i - mals need a hand. Let's

change our roads to help them cross and move on o - ver this land.

Drum

Brid - ges, cul - verts, and o - ver - pas - ses: cross - ings can save us all. It takes

ev - ery crea - ture to make life whole, the large as well as the small.

I am an Elk and I have to trav - el to thrive.

Fol - low - ing the an - cient trail, I'll keep try - ing to stay a - live.

Safe pas - sage: An - i - mals need a hand. Let's

change our roads to help them cross and move on o - ver this land.

Safe   pas - sage: An - i - mals need to   cross!   Let's

change our roads to   save their lives and   share this beau - ti - ful   land.

Find this song on YouTube, and large-format sheet music is available at SmokiesSafePassage.org.

ABOUT THE AUTHOR AND ILLUSTRATOR

FRANCES FIGART grew up in eastern Kentucky where she learned to love living near wildlife. Always a writer and editor, she now directs the Creative Services department at Great Smoky Mountains Association and edits *Smokies Life* magazine, the premier benefit for GSMA members. She is the editor of the 2019 GSMA title, *Back of Beyond: A Horace Kephart Biography*, which won the Thomas Wolfe Memorial Literary Award that same year. She authored a collection of her autobiographical essays, *Seasons of Letting Go: Most of what I know about truly living I learned by helping someone die. A Search for Safe Passage* is her first book for young readers.

EMMA DuFORT hails from west Michigan and visited Great Smoky Mountains National Park frequently as a child. After graduating from Grand Valley State University with a degree in illustration, she returned to live and work in the Smokies. Starting out as a sales assistant in visitor centers run by Great Smoky Mountains Association, she soon became a publications specialist working with GSMA's Creative Services department. Emma has also earned a naturalist certification from Great Smoky Mountains Institute at Tremont. *A Search for Safe Passage* is the first book she has designed and illustrated.